The Poison Tree

The Poison Tree

A Peace Play

Anna Cates

RESOURCE *Publications* · Eugene, Oregon

THE POISON TREE
A Peace Play

Resource Publications
An Imprint of Wipf and Stock Publishers
199 W. 8th Ave., Suite 3
Eugene, OR 97401

www.wipfandstock.com

PAPERBACK ISBN: 978-1-6667-3761-5
HARDCOVER ISBN: 978-1-6667-9726-8
EBOOK ISBN: 978-1-6667-9727-5

APRIL 18, 2022 8:18 AM

For my sweet kitties

"The God of love and peace will be with you."

—*2 COR 13:11, WORLD ENGLISH BIBLE*

Contents

Acknowledgments

The Poison Tree was previously published in eText form by stage-plays.com.

Characters

The Moth Queen: a mysterious agent of divine retribution

Singing Flower 1: a blue-petaled anthropomorphic aster

Singing Flower 2: a yellow-petaled anthropomorphic aster

Singing Flower 3: a rose-petaled anthropomorphic aster

Singing Flower 4: a white-petaled anthropomorphic aster

Hans: Hitler Youth member

Fritz: Hitler Youth member

Herr Wolf: Hitler Youth leader, 30s

Diogenes of Sinope: the classical seeker in toga and garland

Magic Mushroom 1: an anthropomorphic magic mushroom

Magic Mushroom 2: an anthropomorphic magic mushroom

King Elwin: the Elf King

Elder Glorimer: the Elf King's sagacious adviser

Darla: the Elf King's daughter

King Twinklebee: the Fairy King

Buttercup: a consort of the Fairy King

Bluebell: a consort of the Fairy King

Fawn: a consort of the Fairy King

Trixie: a runaway consort of the Fairy King

Babik: a dancing bear from Punjab, Trixie's new companion

Pastor Braun: a troubled pastor, 50s

Dieter: a jewelry thief

Sven: a jewelry thief

Lust: a shadow in the woods

Fear: a shadow in the woods

Despair: a shadow in the woods

Greed: a shadow in the woods

Malice: a shadow in the woods

Pride: a shadow in the woods

Setting

Nazi Germany, the Black Forest, and a parallel fantasy land.

Act I, Scene 1

*(A Hitler Youth camp near the Black Forest: Hans and
Fritz, in Hitler Youth uniforms with swastika armbands,
sneak to the forest's edge. Hans peers behind him, then
furtively removes a pack of cigarettes from his pocket. He
lights one, takes a puff, then hands it to Fritz, who also
takes a puff then coughs uncontrollably. Hans laughs.)*

HANS

Try not to die, Fritz. It's only a cigarette.

(Fritz hands the cigarette back to Hans.)

FRITZ

You can have the rest. I don't care much for tobacco.

HANS

Suit yourself.

FRITZ

(peering into the forest)

Gee, it's dark in the woods.

HANS

Perhaps that's why they call it the Black Forest.

(Hans takes another puff of the cigarette.)

FRITZ

Why do you suppose they don't want us going in there?

HANS

Who knows? Could be erlkings, bad fairies.

FRITZ

(mildly alarmed)

Bad fairies?

HANS

That was a joke, dummy.

FRITZ

Well, my grandmother really believes in fairies. Her grandfather used to hang a star on the barn to ward them away.

HERR WOLF

(approaching from behind)

Hans! Fritz!

HANS

(looks back, alarmed)

It's Herr Wolf!

Act I, Scene 1

(Hans throws his cigarette pack into the bushes, then crushes the lit cigarette beneath his shoe. He swats the air to dissipate the smoke, then moves to another spot.)

HERR WOLF

What are you two doing down here? You were told not to enter the woods.

FRITZ

We were just looking around to see—

HANS

(cutting off Fritz)

We came down here to "answer the call of nature." The latrines are so crowded near suppertime.

FRITZ

(laughing nervously)

Yes, that was why.

HERR WOLF

Hurry up then. But stay near the field, just inside the trees. Some British boys on vacation disappeared near here a few years ago and were never heard from again.

(Herr Wolf thrusts out his hand.)

Heil Hitler!

HANS

(returning the salute)

Sieg Heil!

FRITZ

(returning the salute)

Sieg Heil!

(Fritz watches Herr Wolf walk back to camp, while Hans retrieves his cigarette pack from the bushes and pockets it.)

FRITZ

He's gone!

(Diogenes, dressed in a white toga and green garland, and carrying a lamp, walks through the trees, then disappears from sight.)

HANS

I see someone in the woods! A man in a white robe, carrying a lantern!

FRITZ

(turning)

Where? I don't see a thing.

HANS

I'm sure I saw somebody. Let's find out who!

(Hans starts to move forward, but Fritz grabs him.)

FRITZ

Are you crazy? Didn't you hear Herr Wolf? We can't wander into the forest. Camp rules!

(Hans jerks himself free.)

ACT I, SCENE 1

HANS

So what? My grandfather used to say, "Who you are depends on whether you break the rules like matchsticks or wild horses!"

FRITZ

What's that supposed to mean?

HANS

I've no idea, but it always had a nice ring.

(laughs)

Let's go!

(Hans heads into the woods. Fritz, huffing and puffing and flailing his arms in protest, reluctantly follows.)

FRITZ

I can't believe I'm letting you talk me into this. You always get me into trouble. They'll skin us alive! Or worse!

HANS

Quit bellyaching, you dumb sissy! We need to find this trespasser out. Could be somebody we'll need to report.

FRITZ

(horrified)

A Bolshevist?

HANS

Who knows? That's what we're going to find out.

FRITZ

Maybe you just imagined it.

HANS

I know what I saw: a man in a white robe.

FRITZ

It was probably just some old farmer.

HANS

In a white robe? Farmers don't wear white robes, Fritz. They work with the soil, with manure. They get dirty. Can you imagine slopping hogs in a white robe? Just think for a change!

FRITZ

Maybe it was a ghost of the Great War.

HANS

I don't believe in ghosts.

> (*The light dims, then resumes. Deeper in the woods, the boys pass from tree to tree, looking about. They stop at a clearing with two giant mushrooms, grinning playfully.*)

MAGIC MUSHROOM 1

Eat me!

HANS

Who said that?

MAGIC MUSHROOM 2

Eat me!

ACT I, SCENE 1

FRITZ

Mushrooms!

(The boys draw closer to inspect their find.)

MAGIC MUSHROOM 1

Eat me!

HANS

(to Magic Mushroom 1)

I'm not taking a single bite of you! You're probably poisonous.

MAGIC MUSHROOM 2

Eat me!

MAGIC MUSHROOM 1

I know I'm a pretty big mushroom, and you'd probably have trouble even fitting me in your mouth. But don't let that discourage you.

MAGIC MUSHROOM 2

Eat me!

MAGIC MUSHROOM 1

Eat me!

HANS

Not a chance! You'd probably kill me. My dad warned me about poison mushrooms.

MAGIC MUSHROOM 1

I'm not poison. I'm magic! Eat me!

MAGIC MUSHROOM 2

Eat me!

(Fritz approaches Magic Mushroom 2 and eats a piece of him.)

HANS

What are you doing, idiot? We don't even know these mushrooms!

FRITZ

Too late. I already popped one into my mouth a few trees back, and it was pretty good too. You should try one.

MAGIC MUSHROOM 1

Eat me!

MAGIC MUSHROOM 2

Eat me!

(Fritz pieces off another bite of Magic Mushroom 2. Hans approaches Magic Mushroom 1, picks off a piece of mushroom top, sniffs it, wrinkles his nose, then, warily, tastes it.)

HANS

You're right, Fritz. These are good.

(Magic Mushrooms 1 and 2 giggle as Hans and Fritz stumble forward, intoxicated from the hallucinogenic shrooms. Hans' eyes swim over the constellations.)

HANS

(stupefied)

Oh, mein Gott! Such stars in the heavens! The hazy moon aglow!

FRITZ

(amazed)

Fairy dust sifting down through the trees!

(The mushrooms giggle as the boys fall to the ground in an aura of pixie dust.)

(BLACKOUT)

Act I, Scene 2

(*The Elf King's palace in the woods: King Elwin sits on his throne beside a table, staring into a wine goblet he is stirring into a swirling motion with one hand. He appears troubled, confused over the cup's boding. Elder Glorimer, his senior adviser, enters the room.*)

ELDER GLORIMER

Hail, King Elwin, sovereign of the elves! Might I speak with you?

KING ELWIN

Elder Glorimer? What brings my senior adviser and most trusted confidant into my presence at this hour?

ELDER GLORIMER

Portentous dreams. Peculiar visions. I bring you news, Your Grace, unfortunately, of an unpleasant variety.

(*King Elwin, attentive, leans forward and places his goblet on the table.*)

KING ELWIN

Bad news? I should have known. The wine has turned murky and deep, troubling yet indecipherable. Speak on, Wise One.

ELDER GLORIMER

Strangers from the mortal world have trespassed our borders. Two older boys in military uniforms. I'm afraid they might step on the flowers.

(Upset, King Elwin rises and begins pacing the floor.)

KING ELWIN

This isn't good. This isn't good at all! And I know who's to blame.

ELDER GLORIMER

Your Majesty?

KING ELWIN

The Fairy King! King Twinklebee! *His* kingdom borders the mortal world, not mine. It's *his* responsibility to curtail these invasions.

ELDER GLORIMER

I grieve to see you so upset, Your Grace. How might I council you?

KING ELWIN

This news disappoints but doesn't surprise me. I've grown to expect this from Twinklebee. When a fairy man can't manage his own family, how can he manage the affairs of state?

ELDER GLORIMER

He hails from a long line of wayward sprites, nearly as incompetent as our throttlebottoms, posing as emissaries.

KING ELWIN

Twinklebee has yet to properly wed any of those fag hags he calls wives. And now, the eldest has forsaken him for a dancing bear from Punjab, escaped from a traveling circus!

ELDER GLORIMER

Aha! The wine.

KING ELWIN

I should have seen disaster looming.

ELDER GLORIMER

The boys have eaten magic mushrooms, and God only knows where that might lead them.

KING ELWIN

I am not responsible for the wellbeing of those boys. If they venture into the swamps, if they provoke the Moth Queen . . . I am not accountable for their fate.

(Darla, the Elf King's daughter, peers into the room.)

ELDER GLORIMER

The boys wear a strange insignia on their arm, a broken cross. When I saw it in my dream, I felt a negative tingle.

KING ELWIN

I want those miscreants out of our woods. If Twinklebee wishes to tolerate such misguided souls, he may do so. As for me, I won't see the adulteration of my people or the downfall of our civilization.

ELDER GLORIMER

What is your bidding?

KING ELWIN

Send out scouts. Monitor their steps. If those boys cross the line, arrest them and bring them to me at once.

ELDER GLORIMER

Certainly, Your Majesty.

*(Elder Glorimer bows then leaves.
Darla approaches her father.)*

KING ELWIN

(surprised)

Darla, why aren't you attending to your studies? I hear you're
struggling with astrology.

DARLA

Father, why can't mortals ever enter our lands? King Twinklebee
allows his kindred, on occasion, under certain circumstances, to
consort with them. I've seen them together in the fields, dancing
around bonfires under the moonlight.

KING ELWIN

They turn men into ass-heads for their own merriment! We elves
have at least some scruples.

DARLA

Do you mean that, but for a few toys for children at Christmas, we
largely ignore them? We could do more to influence mortals.

KING ELWIN

Sway them from their wicked ways? Don't be naïve, Darla. If they
won't listen to God, why would they listen to an elf?

DARLA

And yet, King Twinklebee—

KING ELWIN

(cutting Darla off)

Enough with King Twinklebee! You'd compare *me* to that disgraced liege?

DARLA

(amused)

Oh, mercy me! Trixie, the naughty pixie, caught in quite a bear trap, a snare of forbidden love!

(Darla laughs, shaking her head.)

KING ELWIN

You shouldn't laugh, Darla. Some mortals are so ignorant, they can't tell a fairy from an elf. These scandals ruin both our reputations.

DARLA

You're so cynical, Father. Some mortals *do* gain understanding and come to the light.

KING ELWIN

Very few, my peach. Very few.

DARLA

(with a huff)

Why must you always patronize me?

(Darla stomps away.)

KING ELWIN

Darla!

(BLACKOUT)

Act I, Scene 3

(The Fairy King's palace: King Twinklebee, sitting on his bed in stockings, rings a bell, then sets it back on the nightstand.)

KING TWINKLEBEE

(impatiently)

Wives! Wives! Where are my wives?

(Buttercup enters the room.)

KING TWINKLEBEE

Buttercup.

(Bluebell enters the room.)

KING TWINKLEBEE

Bluebell.

(Fawn enters the room.)

KING TWINKLEBEE

Fawn.

BUTTERCUP/BLUEBELL/FAWN

Here we are, my Twinklebee!

KING TWINKLEBEE

(standing)

We're missing somebody. Trixie hasn't returned?

BUTTERCUP

(flirtatiously)

No, My Love. I fear Trixie may be gone for good, but I'm here.

BLUEBELL

Trixie may yet return. What life can she find with that circus beast?

FAWN

I agree with Buttercup. I don't expect we'll ever see Trixie again. She always had a soft spot in her heart for animals.

KING TWINKLEBEE

Then that will be her undoing, though I blame him mostly, and I *will be* avenged for this humiliation.

BUTTERCUP

What are you going to do, My Love?

BLUEBELL

(to King Twinklebee)

Let the vagrancies of the woods have their way with them. Surrender them to fate.

ACT I, SCENE 3

KING TWINKLEBEE

I never surrender!

FAWN

(to King Twinklebee)

Let Trixie go. Forgive.

KING TWINKLEBEE

Never!

BUTTERCUP

I see blood in your eyes, My Love. What are you going to do?

KING TWINKLEBEE

Track them down. I'll place a bear trap beneath every tree in the forest if I must. When I get my hands on that flea-bitten rag of fur from Punjab, I'll . . . I'll . . .

(He begins struggling for words.)

BLUEBELL

(to King Twinklebee)

He'll make a lovely flokati rug.

KING TWINKLEBEE

(to Bluebell)

He'll make an ugly one, but he'll make one nonetheless.

(looking around)

Boots! Boots! Where are my boots?

FAWN

Perhaps you left them in the mudroom.

KING TWINKLEBEE

You all are taking this rather well.

BUTTERCUP

And will you summon your huntsmen to help you track them down?

KING TWINKLEBEE

Not at all. This is a private matter and must be resolved privately, within the family. None should know of Trixie's wanton flight but us. Think how the elves would talk! No, my dears, *you'll* come with me instead.

BLUEBELL

Us? Must you involve us in your violent retribution?

FAWN

I've got it! Why not banish them to the mortal world? That's where that bear came from anyway. If Trixie loves him that much, let her go there with him.

BUTTERCUP

Wonderful idea! Why suffer their blood on our hands? The mortal world is punishment enough. There wars rage.

BLUEBELL

People get sick, grow old, and die.

ACT I, SCENE 3

FAWN

An aura of insanity pervades the mortal world, unlike here.

KING TWINKLEBEE

(reflecting)

You persuade me. Still, we bring our bows and arrows, and plenty of pixie dust for the spell.

BUTTERCUP

Then it is decided.

KING TWINKLEBEE

(spotting his boots beneath the bed)

Aha, my boots!

(He sits on the mattress to shoe himself, then peers up.)

Go! Get ready for the hunt! Why do you just stand there? What are you waiting for? A total eclipse of sun? Go!

(Buttercup, Bluebell, and Fawn hurry off.)

(Blackout)

Act II, Scene 1

(The sun [stage light] shines down on Singing Flowers 1, 2, 3, and 4, blooming on a grassy knoll. They kneel on [or behind a prop of] the hill. They wear petal headdresses and green from the neck down. They sway their heads from side to side, joyfully soaking up the sunlight, singing fa la la la la, etc., or Lamentations 3:22–23.*)

SINGING FLOWERS 1–4
The steadfast love of the Lord never ceases.
His mercies never come to an end.
They are new every morning, new every morning.
Great is your faithfulness, O Lord, great is your faithfulness.

(The light shifts toward a woman's laughter that sounds through the trees. Soon after, Trixie jogs into the clearing.)

TRIXIE
(carefree and happy)

Catch me if you can!

(She hides behind a tree.
Babik, literally dancing, waltzes into the clearing, seeking Trixie.)

---

* English Standard Version.

TRIXIE

(peering out)

Surprise!

BABIK

(embracing Trixie)

You're mine, at last! Mine forever!

(Trixie giggles in his grasp, then loosens from his hold.)

TRIXIE

(toying with his accoutrements)

Oh, Babik! Your ears, your paws, your nose!

BABIK

(wringing his paws bashfully)

Oh, Trixie, you're so fresh, and frisky, and pretty!

*(They offer each other three noisy, close-lipped kisses.
Pastor Braun, wearing dress pants and a shirt with pocket,
walks into the clearing from a new direction. He holds a
case for eyeglasses in one hand. Trixie and Babik don't
at first notice him. Then Trixie sees him over Babik's
shoulder.)*

TRIXIE

(taken off guard)

Oh! There's a man in the woods!

(Babik spins around, placing Trixie behind him.)

PASTOR BRAUN

It's only me, Pastor Braun, your friendly neighborhood reverend. Have you seen a pair of eyeglasses? I lost mine in the woods, and I'm practically blind without them.

BABIK

I know you. You preach at that little chapel. We don't have your eyeglasses, sir.

TRIXIE

(to Pastor Braun)

You shouldn't sneak up like that. It's very alarming.

PASTOR BRAUN

I'm sorry, I . . .

(suddenly irritated by Trixie's attitude)

Well, let me worry about what I need to do, and you can concern yourselves with your own conduct. Just what might you two be doing here, all alone in the deep, dark woods without a chaperone?

BABIK

(jokingly)

We just came here to smell the flowers.

(Trixie breaths in then out, nodding.)

TRIXIE

Ahhh! Yes, that was why.

PASTOR BRAUN

(squinting at them)

I'm not so sure. Your voices sound familiar, but I can't see you clearly without my glasses.

TRIXIE

(pointing)

Maybe you'll find them over there.

BABIK

Ya, I might have seen a pair of glasses way over there

(pointing)

on a patch of moss, or a branch of tree, or something, maybe. Go check it out.

(mumbling to himself)

And make it today and not next week!

PASTOR BRAUN

What was that?

BABIK

Never mind.

PASTOR BRAUN

I'll take a look.

(wagging his finger)

Now, you two behave yourselves.

(Pastor Braun begins to exit.)

TRIXIE

I'm not a child, Pastor Braun, I'm a pixie.

(Pastor Braun exits.
Trixie turns back to Babik.)

TRIXIE

I don't think he recognized us.

BABIK

Good. Now, where were we?

TRIXIE

Perhaps we should move deeper into the woods, find a place more private.

BABIK

Whatever you say, baby!

(Sniggering, hardly able to keep their hands off each other,
they scamper off, Babik's walk like a dance.
From a new direction, Hans and Fritz arrive through the
trees, looking around aimlessly.)

FRITZ

These trees don't look familiar. I think we're lost.

HANS

We're just groggy after those magic mushrooms. We'll find our way back to camp once our heads clear. I hope.

FRITZ

I feel funny, like I've lived here in the woods for a thousand years, yet we've only just arrived.

HANS

It's the mushrooms, Fritz. Snap out of it. Pull yourself together.

FRITZ

I'll never eat another magic mushroom as long as I live, not even if I'm starving. Well, maybe if I'm starving, or maybe even if it's been a very long time since my last meal.

(Fritz licks his lips and sighs.)

HANS

(irritated)

Forget about magic mushrooms! You got your compass with you? I left mine in my tent.

FRITZ

It's right here in my pocket.

(Fritz removes his compass and studies it.)

The needle just keeps spinning round and round! My compass must be broken.

HANS

(snatching the compass)

Let me see that.

(He studies the compass, shakes it, then re-examines it.)

This is weird. Your compass has gone crazy. If it was broken, the needle would freeze in one place, but it just keeps spinning.

FRITZ

What do we do?

HANS

(tossing the compass into the bushes)

Throw this piece of trash away and try to find our way back without it. This way.

(Hans motions to Fritz to follow. They exit.
Herr Wolf enters the clearing from a new direction, looking
left and right.)

HERR WOLF

Hans! Fritz! Hans! Fritz!

(He notes a broken branch.)

I know you've been here. Hans! Fritz! Hans! Fritz!

(He punches his fist into his palm, gnashing his teeth with
rage.)

When I get my hands on you troublemakers, I'll see you in Moringen concentration camp!*

(The Moth Queen flies down through the trees, then lands
on her feet behind Herr Wolf. He turns, startled.)

HERR WOLF

Fraulein! You surprised me. You just came out of nowhere. I wasn't expecting to chance upon a lovely lady all alone in the woods.

(He steps closer.)

THE MOTH QUEEN

I live nearby. And what brings you here?

---

* A Nazi concentration camp for youth.

HERR WOLF

I was looking for two teenage boys. Have you seen any?

THE MOTH QUEEN

Maybe. Maybe not. Why should I tell you? Why do you want to know? Who are you, anyway?

HERR WOLF

(irritated)

I am Wolfgang Wilhelm Wolf, the Third, party member, and you're a bit cheeky. Now tell me what you know. Have you seen two teenage boys? Yes or no? You look like someone with information, cunning as a snake.

THE MOTH QUEEN

(laughs)

Me? I'm innocent as a dove.

HERR WOLF

(grinning, mistaking her for a prostitute, sidling closer, wagging his finger)

Uh-uh—uh-ah! Now you're pretending to be something you're not, but I see through that guise. You're one of these girls who "gets around."

THE MOTH QUEEN

Oh, I've been *everywhere*. When you're the Moth Queen, you just spread your wings and fly!

HERR WOLF

(laughs)

Clever analogy.

(He swats away a few moths flittering near him, then moves closer until he's right beside her.)

You've been bought with a price.

THE MOTH QUEEN

Indeed, I have.

(She touches his swastika armband.)

I begin to understand you, Herr Wolf. You're one of these boys who sometimes steps on the flowers.

HERR WOLF

I'm not a boy, fraulein; I'm a man . . .

THE MOTH QUEEN

You're not more than I can handle.

HERR WOLF

. . . And I dream of boots as broad a snow shoes and as heavy as tanks!

THE MOTH QUEEN

(confident she can take him)

Perhaps we could talk further over bog water and frog song.

HERR WOLF

(ignorant of the danger)

That sounds delightful.

(They exit, arm in arm.)

(BLACKOUT)

Act II, Scene 2

(At the edge of the forest, beside a tree with a carven heart, backdropped by a field and distant church, two robbers arrive to hide stolen loot. Sven carries a box, Dieter two shovels.)

DIETER

Now, where to bury the treasure in these godforsaken wilds?

SVEN

We need a spot we can easily find again.

DIETER

(touching the tree trunk)

Here looks good. Someone carved a heart into the bark of this tree.

(He reads the inscription with one finger.)

"Lise plus Christof."

SVEN

(condescendingly)

Ah, how sweet, a country kissing tree!

DIETER

How about into the ground right below this heart?

SVEN

Hold on, Dieter. We're still rather close to the field and that chapel.

DIETER

All the better. The chapel will be our landmark, just like this tree.

SVEN

What if churchgoers wander over here after the Sunday service? This might be a youth hangout place. Someone might notice the ground disturbed and get suspicious.

DIETER

That old chapel is probably just an abandoned building. Nobody attends church anymore, Sven. Haven't you heard about the new Nazi Party religion with all the fancy new rituals?

SVEN

I just want to make sure we choose the right spot. Need I remind you these are heirloom jewels from the House of Saucson?

(He squeezes the box.)

DIETER

You don't need to remind me. Now, let's start digging.

(He offers Sven a shovel.)

SVEN

(refusing the shovel)

Wait. Let's cut deeper into the woods and look around a bit more. Then, if we find no better spot, we come back here.

DIETER

(frustrated)

How could there be a better spot? But have it your way. We can look a bit further.

(Dieter and Sven, with their jewels and shovels, begin to exit.
Diogenes moves into the clearing from another direction, lamp held aloft. His eyes follow Dieter and Sven's retreat. He shakes his head.)

DIOGENES

(to himself)

Common criminals. How typical! Perhaps in this direction, I'll find an honest man. Poverty is a virtue one can teach oneself.

(He exits, lantern raised.)

(BLACKOUT)

Act II, Scene 3

(In a clearing, an apple tree has borne ripe red fruit. A corpse in ragged clothing is slumped at the tree's base. King Twinklebee, Buttercup, Bluebell, and Fawn walk into the clearing.)

KING TWINKLEBEE
We've reached the border between elven and fairy lands.

BUTTERCUP
It's been ages since I visited this neck of the woods. Here is the old Poison Tree, thankfully, ever dead; only—

BLUEBELL
(cutting off Buttercup)

It's not dead.

FAWN
The Poison Tree has awoken! It has borne bad fruit!

KING TWINKLEBEE
Don't touch it! One of the apples could be for you, and you know what that means.

BUTTERCUP/BLUEBELL/FAWN
Death!

(Buttercup screams, spotting the corpse.)

BUTTERCUP
A corpse lies under the tree!

KING TWINKLEBEE
Someone has eaten the fruit!

BLUEBELL
Who? Fairy or elf?

(King Twinklebee examines the corpse.)

KING TWINKLEBEE
The poison has shriveled and discolored the body beyond recognition.

FAWN
Who would make such vile fruit grow?

BUTTERCUP
Let the villain come forth. I'll put an arrow between his eyes.

(They pace around the tree in dismay, sighing, and wring-ing their hands, etc., trying to make sense of the travesty.)

BLUEBELL
So many apples, oh so many! How could this have happened?

KING TWINKLEBEE

I wish I knew, but right now we have only unanswered questions.

FAWN

What are we going to do?

BUTTERCUP

The tree must be axed down.

KING TWINKLEBEE

We cannot remedy this offense ourselves. Only elves are so gifted. They excel at wood cutting, carving, and tinker toy making. Those are elf, not fairy, skills.

BLUEBELL

Should we change our present course and notify King Elwin?

FAWN

He won't be pleased.

KING TWINKLEBEE

I won't be King Elwin's harbinger of ill tidings. I'm no messenger boy, and you know how difficult he can be. He'll find out soon enough through his own devices. But we should pause and review our objectives in light of this unexpected development.

BUTTERCUP

Yes, if the Poison Tree has awoken and taken life, other evils may be lurking in the woods.

KING TWINKLEBEE

I feel the threat of a great shadow.

BLUEBELL

Trixie is out there, somewhere, all alone with that bear! We must find her, warn her, and bring her home.

FAWN

Her giddy heart could be blind to any danger.

BUTTERCUP

They might wander to this very spot and eat the fruit. There could be apples here for both of them.

BLUEBELL

(growing hysterical)

What if the apples rot into the earth, seep into the ground water, and poison the drinking supply? Oh, this is terrible, terrible!

KING TWINKLEBEE

(to Bluebell)

Silence! Give me peace to gather my thoughts and muster my strength.*

FAWN

What now, Twinklebee?

KING TWINKLEBEE

Finding Trixie can no longer be our aim. She's on her own now. Instead, we hunt down the fiend who revived this tree. After me!

(The fairies exit, King Twinklebee in the lead.)

(BLACKOUT)

---

* Optional song here.

Act II, Scene 4

(Hand in hand, Trixie and Babik arrive at a new location in the forest. As is typical, Babik dances as his walks. They stop to survey their surroundings: mountains and forests.)

TRIXIE

What beautiful scenery! Mountains and forests as far as the eye can see.

BABIK

Sure beats littered asphalt beyond iron bars.

TRIXIE

Forget your past. Forget your pain. It is no more. You're with me now.

BABIK

Whatever you say, baby!

TRIXIE

In all my life, I've never felt happier.

> *(sobering)*

And yet, I fear storm clouds loom on the horizon.

BABIK

How so? Speak your mind. We musn't keep secrets from each other.

TRIXIE

We escaped your captors and the crowds. But now what? Where do we go in this vast wilderness? Where do we call home?

BABIK

Anywhere you want, baby. I'll build us a cabin in the woods. We'll feast on fresh fish and wild honey and live happily ever after.

TRIXIE

What about Twinklebee? We're not out of the woods yet. I fear a bounty rests on our heads, burning down like hot coals. I fear, in the end, all our scheming will come to grief.

BABIK

Cast your fears aside, baby. I can take down that blowfly!

(Babik boxes the air, causing Trixie to giggle.)

BABIK

Besides, God will make a way. In my darkest hour at the hands of my captors, when my toes were bloody from endless nights of dancing in smoke-filled circus tents, there you were, Trixie. You picked the lock of my cage and brought me to this beautiful place. I don't doubt what God can do.*

(Blackout)

---

* Optional song here.

Act III, Scene 1

(The Elf King's palace in the woods: King Elwin sits on his throne, staring into a wine goblet.
Elder Glorimer enters the room.)

ELDER GLORIMER

Hail, King Elwin!

KING ELWIN

Elder Glorimer. I was wanting to talk to you. The wine is dark and thick like blood. It bodes a sign. Tell me, you who are so gifted, what does it mean?

ELDER GLORIMER

I wish I'd better news, Your Grace. Those boys I spoke of not long ago?

KING ELWIN

What of them?

ELDER GLORIMER

They aren't the only trespassers in our lands. Another mortal has followed them here, to retrieve them, it would seem. He appears a leader among mortals, though a lesser one.

KING ELWIN

Fiery fiddlesticks! Any others?

ELDER GLORIMER

At least two. Thieves with stolen jewels, who've found a supposedly clandestine spot to hide their loot, though I've divined exactly where it is, down in the valley.

KING ELWIN

We must confiscate those jewels.

ELDER GLORIMER

All in good time, Your Grace. I'd council you to first attend to the peril the mortals pose. I doubt the thieves know the boys or their leader, though all threaten our security.

KING ELWIN

(rising from his throne to pace)

Where are these undesirables coming from?

ELDER GLORIMER

I've discerned that the barrier separating our world from the mortal world has cracked open at an undeterminable location. An invasion of epic proportions awaits us unless we act quick to heal the breach.

> (Darla peers into the room, then discreetly enters to listen
> to the enfolding conversation.)

Act III, Scene 1

KING ELWIN

How did this happen? That dome has ever protected us, sheltered us from the outside world and all its harms and defilements. How?

ELDER GLORIMER

I can't say for sure. Perhaps a bomb exploding. Maybe a demon.

KING ELWIN

We can exorcise demons. We'll chant the sacred prayers, enact the sacred rites.

ELDER GLORIMER

There's more.

KING ELWIN

Dread fills me already, but speak on.

ELDER GLORIMER

The ancient Poison Tree has awoken.

KING ELWIN

No!

ELDER GLORIMER

It has borne bad fruit. Its boughs sag with fat red apples!

KING ELWIN

No!

ELDER GLORIMER

And, a dead body lies beneath it.

DARLA

The invasion from the mortal world must be to blame.

KING ELWIN

(stunned with dismay)

The Poison Tree has awoken and taken a life?

(clutching his heart)

My heart revisits an ancient woe that has grieved me since my childhood.

(soberly singing "I Heard the Bells on Christmas Day")

I heard the bells on Christmas day
Their old familiar carols play
And mild and sweet their songs repeat
Of peace on Earth good will to men

(notably more grieved)

But in despair I bowed my head
There is no peace on Earth I said
For hate is strong and mocks the song
Of peace on Earth, good will to men . . .

(King Elwin's voice breaks with despair.)

ELDER GLORIMER

(boldly reciting, not singing, more lines from the carol)

God is not dead, nor does he sleep.
The wrong shall fail, the right prevail
with peace on Earth good will to men . . .

Your Grace, there are those who in times of crisis flounder, but you cannot. You must be strong and take courage. Your people need you.

DARLA

The world needs you.*

KING ELWIN

Why do you doubt me? Fear doesn't grip me. I'm already engaged.
I know what I must do. I must chop down the Poison Tree. Only, I
need a magic axe. Where do I find one?

(Momentarily, all three just stare at each other.)

KING ELWIN/ELDER GLORIMER/DARLA

The Moth Queen!

ELDER GLORIMER

The Moth Queen is insatiable when it comes to violent men. Her
stash of weapons from her former meals should supply us with a
magic axe.

(with sudden doubts)

Hopefully.

(BLACKOUT)

---

* Optional song here.

Act III, Scene 2

(The Moth Queen's lair in the swamps is like a cross be-
tween a shanty and open campsite, or like a rustic pavilion
with a floor, but without walls, that blends into, and
harmonizes with, nature. Visible: an empty throne and
treasure chest, and a door for guests to knock. Pots, pans,
and camping gear hang from pegs.
Little moths flitter through the air and pester and nip at
Herr Wolf, tied at the wrists and ankles with ropey vines
against a cluster of trees, serving as a substitute back wall
of the set-up. His Nazi uniform is dirty and torn. Raw red
wounds show beneath giant moth holes, eaten into his uni-
form. Face dirty and beaten, hair disheveled, he struggles
in his binds, enraged.)

HERR WOLF

(to the moths)

Get away from me, you insufferable pests!

(looking for the Moth Queen in vain)

Where are you? Untie me at once!

(He growls in anger and continues to thrash.
Hans and Fritz peer through the bushes. Their mouths fall
open when they behold Herr Wolf.)

FRITZ

(whispering to Hans)

It's Herr Wolf! What do we do?

HANS

Look at the size of those moth holes! It must be that thing we saw flying over the bog!

FRITZ

This is our fault, Hans. Herr Wolf must have come here looking for us. We should help him.

> *(Fritz moves forward, but Hans jerks him back by a fistful of Nazi Youth uniform.)*

HANS

Let him rot! We need to get out of here, fast, before that thing returns, or we'll be her next meal.

> *(The Moth Queen slips out from the shadows.)*

FRITZ

There she is!

> *(Hans places one finger to his mouth, then continues to watch. The moths leave Herr Wolf. The Moth Queen reaches out one hand to help them congregate about her.)*

THE MOTH QUEEN

(to her moths)

Hello, my sweeties, my pretty babies. Did you have plenty to eat? Was Herr Wolf a tasty snack?

> *(She laughs.)*

I see you've left plenty for me.

HERR WOLF

(enraged)

This is outrageous! Release me, you she-devil!

(The Moth Queen inspects her prey, strutting about, arms folded. Herr Wolf struggles in his binds, but they hold him fast.)

HERR WOLF

You try my patience, fraulein. This is your final warning. Untie me at once!

(An eerie mothy noise emanates from the Moth Queen. Herr Wolf shows alarm.)

HERR WOLF

What was that?

(Hans and Fritz watch, horrified, as the Moth Queen takes to flight, plunging onto Herr Wolf, who screams pitifully.)

HANS

Run!

(Hans and Fritz dive back into the forest.)

(BLACKOUT)

Act III, Scene 3

(A peaceful clearing, deep in the forest: suddenly, male screams sound from somewhere hidden behind bramble. Growls from a bear join the screaming. Babik runs into the clearing, blood dripping from his mouth.)

BABIK

Oh no! Oh no! What have I done? What have I done? I've killed them, killed them both! Not good men by any means, but still human beings. Oh!

(He peers behind him where he's left behind Dieter and Sven's dead bodies.)

I've always been such a nice, peaceful animal. But what's a bear to do when such menacing foes invade one's territory? Especially when they lift their shovels like that, ready to attack! Oh! That's what big bears do: fight back!

TRIXIE

(her voice drifting in from a hidden location)

Babik? Babik? Where are you, my sweet Teddy?

BABIK

Oh no! It's Trixie!

TRIXIE

(still hidden by the copse)

Where's my big, beautiful bear cub?

BABIK

(examining his palms)

Oh no! There's blood on my paws! I can't let Trixie see me like this.

(Babik dances away in anguish. Soon after, Trixie walks into in the clearing, looking about for Babik.)

TRIXIE

Babik? Babik?

(growing more impatient)

Okay, Babik, this isn't funny. Come out; come out, wherever you are!

(She peers behind trees then bushes, looking for him.)

Where did he go? Babik? Babik?

(In a huff, she exits in the opposite direction as Babik.)

(Blackout)

Act IV, Scene 1

(Somewhere in the wilderness, a tired Hans and Fritz stumble along, their uniforms now a bit shabby. Fritz notices some raspberry bushes.)

FRITZ

Raspberries!

HANS

Great! I'm starving!

(They hasten to the bush and begin eating the berries.)

FRITZ

(chewing)

Not bad.

HANS

We've had nothing but mushrooms, frogs' legs, and walnuts since we first got here.

FRITZ

Too bad there isn't more, even though these are mostly gone by.

HANS

Don't drop any.

(Diogenes moves into view, lantern held aloft.
Wolfing down berries, Hans and Fritz don't at first see
him.)

DIOGENES

(clearing his throat)

Ahem.

(Startled, Hans and Fritz spin around.)

HANS

Who are you?

DIOGENES

I was about to ask you the same question, strangers in the woods.
I'm Diogenes of Sinope . . .

FRITZ

What part of Germany is that?

DIOGENES

. . . And a citizen of the world.

HANS

You're the man in the white robe!

DIOGENES

Where I come from, we call it a "toga."

FRITZ

(to Diogenes)

We came here looking for you.

DIOGENES

How ironic. I usually find myself the seeker among men.

FRITZ

(to Diogenes)

And now we're lost in the woods.

DIOGENES

Two lost boys? A familiar tale. The world is full of them.

(Hans whips a switchblade out of his pocket and points it at Diogenes. He totters on his feet, ready to get violent.)

HANS

These are *our* raspberries. We've claimed this bush, so stand back before things get nasty.

DIOGENES

Put the knife away, young man. It isn't berries I seek. I seek an honest man, a good man. I've scoured the earth, it seems an eternity, yet I find nothing. Nobody. Not a single righteous soul. Only endless shadows within my persistent hope.

HANS

If you haven't figured out by now it's Herr Hitler, you're either stupid, bad, or crazy.

FRITZ

(nodding)

Ya!

DIOGENES

It isn't madness you see in me, young man. My head is just a little different from yours. I'm sick of brutes and beasts. I seek a true human being.

FRITZ

What's the use of seeking if you can't find what you're looking for?

HANS

Ya, why don't you just give up?

DIOGENES

I would have, long ago, were there not some meaning in the mystery, a force I cannot comprehend that compels me. Some divine presence holds me in tow.*

HANS

(putting his knife away)

Well, if you're not here to steal our berries . . .

DIOGENES

(leaning in to scrutinize them more closely)

Who did you say you were again? I didn't catch your names?

---

* Optional song here.

FRITZ

I'm Fritz, and he's Hans. We're members of the Hitler Youth, the Fuhrer says, the hope of the future.

HANS/FRITZ

(hands forward)

Heil Hitler!

DIOGENES

(stepping back)

Oh, horrible! Now I see it: the end of worlds! Doom and despair! Blood! Blood on every horizon!

(He reels away from the boys.)

I must move on. Perhaps in this direction, I'll find the one I seek.

(Lamp lifted, Diogenes hastens away.)

FRITZ

I'm not sure he meant that as a compliment.

HANS

What a dope. Only a moron wears poison ivy in his hair.

(Hans ducks as an arrow whizzes by his head. Suddenly, King Twinklebee, Buttercup, Bluebell, and Fawn surround the boys with raised bows.)

KING TWINKLEBEE

Halt! Hand over your weapons, and put your hands up.

(Hans and Fritz raise their hands.)

HANS

We don't have any weapons.

FRITZ

We were just eating some berries, no harm done.

BUTTERCUP

His Majesty, King Twinklebee, will be the judge of that.

KING TWINKLEBEE

(to Hans)

Don't lie to me. I saw that blade glinting through the leaves. You pointed it at that peaceful pilgrim. Now hand it over.

(Irritated, Hans removes his switchblade from his pocket and gives it to King Twinklebee.)

HANS

A good knife comes in handy when you're lost in the woods.

KING TWINKLEBEE

(to Fritz)

You too.

(Fritz removes his knife from his pocket and forfeits it. King Twinklebee turns to Buttercup.)

KING TWINKLEBEE

Frisk them.

(While Bluebell and Fawn keep their arrows raised, King Twinklebee and Buttercup lower their guard. Buttercup frisks Hans and Fritz, then explores their pockets.)

ACT IV, SCENE 1

BUTTERCUP

Nothing else but a few coins.

(She hands the coins to King Twinklebee, who pockets the tender.)

KING TWINKLEBEE

(to Hans and Fritz)

You are neither elf nor fairy, nor does any magic abide with you. Who are you, and where did you come from?

HANS

We're from a nearby village, a farming community.

KING TWINKLEBEE

Not since the Napoleonic Wars have mortals penetrated our midst, though we do at times enter your lands, if only to buy a child's tooth. How did you get here?

HANS

I've no idea, honestly.

FRITZ

We were warned not to enter the woods, but we did it anyway. It was his idea!

(Hans grimaces with annoyance at Fritz.)

HANS

We entered the woods to look for that man in the white robe, but now we're lost. We need to get back to our camp, but our compass broke. If you'll kindly show us the way out of these wilds, we'll gladly be on our way.

KING TWINKLEBEE

You've lied to me before, so I've little reason to trust you. And that you'd arrive exactly when the Poison Tree awakens bodes ill for you both. That cannot be mere coincidence.

(King Twinklebee meets the gazes of the other fairies, who mummer and gasp at his logic.)

BLUEBELL

It was them.

FAWN

You two have been very naughty boys.

BUTTERCUP

Guilty dogs.

TWINKLEBEE

Fiends.

HANS

Nein! We've been good.

FRITZ

We've marched in line.

HANS

We've sung in turn.

FRITZ

We've hailed the Fuhrer.

HANS/FRITZ

We've been model citizens.

BLUEBELL

Rubbish!

KING TWINKLEBEE

Lies!

HANS

You're crazy! All of you, all of this, is just crazy!

(The fairies circle about them.)

KING TWINKLEBEE

(circling the boys)

You were angry at a foe. You told it not, your wrath did grow.

BUTTERCUP

(circling the boys)

And you watered it in fears, night and morning with your tears.

BLUEBELL

(circling the boys)

And you sunned it with smiles, and with soft deceitful wiles.

FAWN

(circling the boys)

And it grew both day and night. Till it bore an apple bright.

KING TWINKLEBEE

(circling the boys)

And your foe beheld it shine, and he ate it, didn't he?

HANS

I don't know what you're talking about.

FRITZ

We didn't know there was an apple orchard nearby. We were just—

KING TWINKLEBEE

(cutting off Fritz)

Silence! Speak not unless you're spoken to.

BUTTERCUP

And were you glad to see your foe outstretched beneath that tree?

BLUEBELL

Did you dance a merry jig?

FAWN

Did you chortle with glee?

KING TWINKLEBEE

(to his consorts)

Enough! If we're to interrogate these suspects properly, we must arrest them and take them into custody.

(to Hans and Fritz)

Turn around.

(They turn. King Twinklebee rips off their Nazi armbands.)

Act IV, Scene 1

KING TWINKLEBEE

I'll take these.

HANS

(appalled)

What are you doing? The swastika is more powerful than death!

KING TWINKLEBEE

Your foul emblems mean nothing here. Now march forward, hands up!

(Goaded by pointed arrows, Hans and Fritz, hands raised, leave the clearing, followed by the fairies.)

(Blackout)

Act IV, Scene 2

(Accompanied by many moths in her lair by the swamps, the Moth Queen sits cross-legged on her thrown, cleaning her teeth with a toothpick.
King Elwin, Elder Glorimer, and Darla come calling. King Elwin knocks on the door with his scepter: rap, tap, tap! The Moth Queen throws her toothpick in the trash then learns forward in her seat.)

THE MOTH QUEEN

Who is it?

KING ELWIN

King Elwin and company.

THE MOTH QUEEN

Oh! Coming!

(The Moth Queen hastens to the door and lets them in.)

What a pleasant surprise, Your Majesty. Come in.

KING ELWIN

(leaning forward to kiss her hand)

The pleasure is mine, Milady.

(Darla curtsies.)

ELDER GLORIMER

(bowing to the Moth Queen)

Your Majesty.

THE MOTH QUEEN

Forgive the disarray. I wasn't expecting you, and I've had little time to tidy up since my last meal.

(She places a hand on her abdomen as if to say, "Indigestion.")

Now, what can I do for my elfish allies?

ELDER GLORIMER

Pardon our intrusion, Your Grace. We come in an hour of need, seeking assistance in a matter of grave importance.

THE MOTH QUEEN

You frighten me, Elder Glorimer. What's wrong?

KING ELWIN

Time is wasting, so I'll skip to the point. The Poison Tree of old has awoken, and a dead body lies beneath its accursed branches.

THE MOTH QUEEN

No! That cannot be! How? Who?

ELDER GLORIMER

Some evil force has broken the dome protecting us from the mortal world, allowing entry all manner of questionable flesh.

THE MOTH QUEEN

Could likely have been my last meal.

KING ELWIN

Let's hope so, but the breach must be mended.

ELDER GLORIMER

And the Poison Tree, which has borne bad fruit, cut down.

THE MOTH QUEEN

How do I fit in?

KING ELWIN

We need a magic axe. Do you have one?

THE MOTH QUEEN

Possibly. Stand back.

(The elves step aside as the Moth Queen pushes a large chest into the center of the floor. She kneels behind it.)

In this chest, I keep my collection of weapons, confiscated from my previous meals.

(She opens the lid and removes a candelabra.)

Candelabra?

KING ELWIN

No. We need a magic axe.

ACT IV, SCENE 2

THE MOTH QUEEN

(removing a lead pipe)

Lead pipe?

ELDER GLORIMER

A magic axe, Your Majesty.

THE MOTH QUEEN

(removing a noose)

Noose?

(She places it on the floor beside the chest.)

I know. That's not what you're looking for. Let me see . . . a magic axe . . .

(She rummages through the chest.)

I've got cannonballs, boomerangs, bludgeons, bombs, crow bars, iron maidens, spears, every kind of knife, bow, sword, and gun forged by man . . .

DARLA

Surely, you have a magic axe somewhere in that bottomless pit.

THE MOTH QUEEN

Aha! An axe!

(She removes the murder weapon from the chest.)

ELDER GLORIMER

Is it a *magic* axe?

THE MOTH QUEEN

It could be, possibly. But you'll have to say the magic words.

KING ELWIN

Please. And *thank you.*

THE MOTH QUEEN

(rolling her eyes)

That's not what I meant!

ELDER GLORIMER

(to King Elwin)

I think Her Majesty means us to recite the *Lord's Prayer.*

DARLA

An *Our Father!*

KING ELWIN

Together now.

DARLA/THE MOTH QUEEN/
ELDER GLORIMER/KING ELWIN*

Our Father, which art in Heaven,
Hallowed be Thy Name.
Thy kingdom come.
Thy will be done on Earth,
As it is in Heaven.
Give us this day our daily bread.
And forgive us our debts,
As we forgive our debtors.
And lead us not into temptation,
But deliver us from evil.
For thine is the kingdom,
And the power, and the glory,
Forever. Amen.

* The characters could also sing the song version of this prayer as a quartet.

THE MOTH QUEEN

Oh! I felt something: A magical tingle just entered my hand then penetrated the axe. This should do.

(She hands King Elwin the axe.)

ELDER GLORIMER

Many thanks, Your Grace. What would we do without you?

THE MOTH QUEEN

(waving them away)

Go! Go! Cut down that Poison Tree, and God speed you!

(The elves head for the door.)

THE MOTH QUEEN

Wait! There's one more thing.

(The elves turn back.)

ELDER GLORIMER

(to the Moth Queen)

Your Grace?

THE MOTH QUEEN

Be warned. Shadows have entered the woods. But they are only shadows, with no power to harm you, unless you give in to them, which you must not do, or face catastrophic consequences.

KING ELWIN

We are warned, Milady. We won't give in to the shadows.

(BLACKOUT)

Act IV, Scene 3

(A prison cell in a castle tower: moonlight glints through a barred window.
Fritz, dismayed, sits on a ragged cot, head in his hands.
Hans paces the cell, frustrated, mumbling, hands fisting.
Fritz peers up.)

FRITZ

Imagine, I could be home right now, my feet by the fireplace, enjoying Mutter's stuffed cabbage, with apple strudel for dessert. Instead, here I am, rotting in this jail cell.

HANS

Oh, shut up, you big cry baby! We need to think our way out of this mess, and that means *I* need to concentrate.

FRITZ

I knew this would happen. Every time I hang out with you, I get into trouble.

HANS

(ceasing pacing)

You think this is my fault?

ACT IV, SCENE 3

FRITZ

It was your idea to come here. You had to hunt down that mysterious man in the white robe. Big mistake!

HANS

That's what you think? That this is my fault?

FRITZ

You should have kept your knife in your pocket.

HANS

You should have kept your mouth shut and let me do the talking.

(mocking Fritz's previous comments to the fairies)

"We were warned not to enter the woods, but we did it anyway." Those fairies didn't need to know that, Fritz! That was none of their business.

FRITZ

(rising from the cot)

You lied about having a knife. They were spying on us the whole time. They saw your knife. They knew you had one. They might have trusted us more if you hadn't proven yourself a liar.

HANS

I was right to try to keep ahold of that knife. We needed those knives to survive in the woods. You know, Fritz, there's one thing about you I just don't understand: how your head measured up one of the biggest in the class. Must be a thick skull. Beneath all those layers of bone, your brain's not but the size of a pea.

(Fritz, losing his temper, punches Hans in the face.)

FRITZ

I'm not so stupid I don't know when you need a fist in the face!

(Hans, stunned, touches his smarting mouth, then rushes forward in a rage, grabs Fritz, and smashes his head against the window. The iron bars creak open as a unit. Fritz groans then falls down on the cot.)

HANS

(examining the broken window)

Wonderful! I love you, Fritz! There's a purpose for that thick skull after all!

FRITZ

(rubbing his sore head)

What are you talking about?

HANS

(touching the crumbled rock)

This old castle seems a bit crumbly here and there. Your head just broke through the window!

FRITZ

(rising from the cot and seeing the open window)

We're free!

(Fritz jumps up and down excitedly.)

HANS

(Hans peers out the window.)

Not yet. It's a *long* jump down, but I think we can make it. Hurry! Let's get out of here before Herr Fairy Man returns with his thumb screws!

(Hans then Fritz jump out the window.)

(BLACKOUT)

Act IV, Scene 4

(The sun [stage light] shines down on singing Flowers 1, 2, 3, and 4, blooming on a hill with a stump, singing fa la la la la, etc., or Psalm 57:9-11.*)

SINGING FLOWERS 1-4

I will give thanks to you, O Lord, among the peoples.
I will sing praises to you among the nations.
For your steadfast love is great, is great to the heavens,
And your faithfulness, your faithfulness, to the clouds.
Be exalted, O God, above the heavens.
Let your glory be over all the Earth.
Be exalted, O God, above the heavens.
Let your glory, let your glory, let your glory be over all the Earth.

SINGING FLOWER 1

(breathing in deeply)

Ah, what wonderful sunshine!

SINGING FLOWER 2

Bless my soul, I must have grown an inch in a week!

---

* English Standard Version.

SINGING FLOWER 3

(tauntingly)

You always were a cornstalk!

(Singing Flowers 1, 3, and 4 snigger. Trixie walks through the trees, then stops by the flowers.)

TRIXIE

I thought I heard *a racket* over here.

SINGING FLOWER 1

What's put you in such bad spirits?

TRIXIE

You wouldn't understand. You're a flower, and I'm a fairy.

SINGING FLOWER 2

I suspect you might be looking for that bear?

TRIXIE

(suddenly excited)

Was he here?

SINGING FLOWER 3

Not long ago.

SINGING FLOWER 4

But he ran off toward the mountain in a terrible hurry.

(Trixie, sulking, sits down on the stump.)

TRIXIE

He said he loved me. Why would he abandon me?

SINGING FLOWER 1

Who can tell? Bears will be bears.

SINGING FLOWER 2

He may have gotten himself into trouble.

TRIXIE

I can't lose Babik. He's all I've got. What should I do?

SINGING FLOWER 3

Just bloom!

SINGING FLOWER 4

Bloom!

SINGING FLOWER 1

Bloom wherever you're planted!

SINGING FLOWER 2

Just bloom!

TRIXIE

What's that supposed to mean? I'm not sure we speak the same language.

ACT IV, SCENE 4

SINGING FLOWER 3

Well, some flowers bloom in a bright open field, others in a deep, dark forest where only the faintest patches of sunlight filter down through the leaves.

(Trixie hops off the stump, frustrated.)

TRIXIE

Why am I even talking to you? This is hopeless!

(Trixie starts to leave.)

SINGING FLOWER 4

Watch out! Don't step on the flowers!

(Trixie disappears into the copse.)

SINGING FLOWER 1

Poor Trixie.

SINGING FLOWER 2

She's fighting an uphill battle.

SINGING FLOWER 3

With herself.

SINGING FLOWER 4

Shhh! No idle chatter. Here comes Pastor Braun!

(Pastor Braun emerges from the brush. He holds his eye-glasses case in one hand and uses the other to feel his way among the branches. He stops by the flowers.)

PASTOR BRAUN

Ah! I may not see very well without my spectacles, but I can still recognize the fresh scent of forest flowers. How lovely!

(*The Singing Flowers duck their heads, bashfully, smiling at each other from side to side. Pastor Braun touches the stump.*)

PASTOR BRAUN

Good. I thought that might be a tree stump.

(*He sits down to ease his aching back and catch his breath. He removes a handkerchief from his pocket and wipes his sweated face, then repockets it.*)

Dear God, I don't know how much more of this wandering in the wilderness I can take.

(*He twists from side to side, groaning, trying to ease the crick in his back.*

A shadow emerges from the copse. The shadow is covered, head to toe, in a black material, revealing only the silhouette of a woman. Pastor Braun peers her way.*)

PASTOR BRAUN

Lust! What a surprise. It's been a while.

(*She sidles seductively toward him, stops behind him, and slides her fingers across his shoulders. He recoils.*)

PASTOR BRAUN

Not now, Lust. I'm too overburdened with moral dilemmas at present. Find someone else to pester.

(*Persistent, still behind him, she draws little circles through his hair with one finger. He swats her hand.*)

PASTOR BRAUN

Stop that! You can be incredibly annoying.

(He rises from the stump while Lust backs off.)

PASTOR BRAUN

That's right. Just go away!

(Lust raises both hands and slowly steps back to the tree line, still facing him. Pastor Braun sits back down on the stump. Another shadow steps out from the copse right beside Lust. Pastor Braun turns their way.)

PASTOR BRAUN

Returned with a friend, have you?

(Lust gestures toward the new shadow as if to introduce the new male silhouette, also covered in black.)

PASTOR BRAUN

Oh, Fear. That's what I was afraid of!

(Pastor Braun quivers with fright. Another shadow in male silhouette steps forward on the other side of Lust.)

PASTOR BRAUN

Despair! You too? Why can't you all just leave me be?

(The trio inches toward him. Pastor Braun picks up a stick and hops off the stump.)

PASTOR BRAUN

I won't give in to you.

(Despair takes another step forward. Pastor Braun becomes enraged, screaming.)

PASTOR BRAUN

Go! Leave me! I won't have you! I won't have any of you!

*(He throws the stick at them. They dart back into the forest
and disappear. Pastor Braun lifts his head.)*

PASTOR BRAUN

Oh, my God, my God, why have you led me into this dark wilderness, so full of shadows?

(reciting Psalm Five*)

Give ear to my words, O Lord, consider my meditation.
Hearken unto the voice of my cry, my King, and my God:
For unto thee will I pray.
My voice shalt thou hear in the morning,
O Lord; in the morning will I direct my prayer
Unto thee, and will look up.

SINGING FLOWER 1

I hate to interrupt your meditation, Pastor Braun, but the glasses
you seek are in your hand.

*(Pastor Braun peers down and opens the eyeglasses case.
He shakes his head with a smile.)*

PASTOR BRAUN

So they are.

*(He puts on his glasses, then places the case in his shirt
pocket.)*

---

* Pastor Braun could also sing the song version of Psalm Five.

ACT IV, SCENE 4

Thank you. That helps considerably.

> *(Hans and Fritz, still in uniform but without their swastika armbands, step out from the trees. Singing Flower 1 clears her throat and tilts her head toward the boys. Pastor Braun turns then jumps.)*

SINGING FLOWER 2

Frightening, I know.

SINGING FLOWER 3

But if you'd only just talk to them, maybe they'd see the light.

PASTOR BRAUN

Of course. That's next on my daily agenda.

> *(He adjusts his glasses, grins broadly, then swaggers over to Fritz and Hans. He holds out his hand for a handshake.)*

Hello. I'm Pastor Braun.

> *(He shakes Hans' hand.)*

HANS

Hans.

FRITZ

> *(shaking Pastor Braun's hand)*

Fritz.

(BLACKOUT)

Act V: Scene 1

(In the clearing with the Poison Tree, a dead vulture lies on the ground where the corpse had been. Only a few rags of the deceased remain.

King Elwin, axe in hand, enters the clearing, with Elder Glorimer and Darla following for moral support. King Elwin gasps when he beholds the tree.)

KING ELWIN

So it's true. The Poison Tree lives. Only, I wasn't expecting so many apples.

ELDER GLORIMER

How deceitfully sweet they seem. Red, ripe, and crisp.

(Elder Glorimer prods the dead vulture with his staff, then picks it up.)

It would seem vultures ate the body and became poisoned themselves.

DARLA

Throw it away!

(Elder Glorimer tosses the dead vulture into the bushes, then wipes his hand on his garments. King Elwin picks up a rag.)

KING ELWIN

A few scraps of clothing are all that remain of the deceased. May he rest in peace.

DARLA

Let's hope that magic axe works.

(A shadow, in the silhouette of a woman, emerges from the copse.)

DARLA

Oh, no! We've got company.

(The shadow strides up to King Elwin and places her hand on the axe, then tries to tug it out of his grasp.)

KING ELWIN

Just what do you think you're doing? This magic axe doesn't belong to you. Now hands off!

(struggling with the shadow for the axe)

I know you want it, Greed, but you can't have it.

ELDER GLORIMER

Let go of the axe, Greed.

DARLA

It's one of the shadows the Moth Queen warned us about. Don't let her have the axe!

KING ELWIN

(struggling)

I wouldn't dream of it.

(But the struggle continues.)

DARLA

(to Greed)

Let go of the axe!

ELDER GLORIMER

(to Greed)

Let go, and begone!

KING ELWIN

(struggling)

You two don't seem to realize just how greedy. Greed. Really. *Is!*

DARLA

Perhaps I can be of help.

(Darla grabs Greed from behind and tries to pry her away. With additional help from Elder Glorimer, Greed finally loosens her grip on the axe.)

ELDER GLORIMER

Be off!

(Elder Glorimer tosses Greed into the bushes. She returns with a new shadow, in male silhouette.)

ELDER GLORIMER

(snarling at the new shade)

Malice! I have ever despised you.

DARLA

Don't give in, Father! Don't give in to the shadows!

KING ELWIN

(to Malice)

I can see why one such as you would haunt a poison tree, but you won't stop me from chopping it down. Best you return to the darkness from whence you came.

(Greed and Malice lunge forward. The struggle renews between Greed and King Elwin and begins between Elder Glorimer and Malice.)

ELDER GLORIMER

Away with you!

(He hurls Malice back into the copse.)

KING ELWIN

Go!

(He hurls Greed back into the copse.)

DARLA

Hurry and chop down the tree. It gives life to the shadows. When the tree is gone, so too will the shadows be.

ELDER GLORIMER

Darla is right. Take down the tree now before a whole army of shades descends upon us.

(Darla and Elder Glorimer step back while King Elwin hunches beside the tree to chop it down.)

KING ELWIN

Here it goes. One, two, three . . .

(He draws back the axe, then freezes as he beholds a new shadow emerge from the copse. The new shade, in silhouette of a man, is gigantic compared to the other shades.)

KING ELWIN

Oh, no. Pride. I feel a weakness in my knees.

(King Elwin stands still, wilted, while Pride steps forward.)

PRIDE

You resisted the others, but you won't resist me.

ELDER GLORIMER

Don't listen to him, Your Majesty. You can conquer Pride. I think. I hope.

(doubtingly)

Darla?

DARLA

Tell him where he can go, Daddy!

KING ELWIN

(smiling foolishly)

Hello, Pride. It's me, King Elwin.

(The axe falls to the ground. King Elwin stretches out his hand for a handshake while Pride, laughing, draws near. Darla screams with dismay.)

DARLA

No!

PRIDE

Bow down at my feet, King Elwin, and worship me!

ELDER GLORIMER

Pride cannot be your cohort, Your Majesty. Now pick up the axe and chop down the tree.

(King Elwin tries to shake away his stupor.)

KING ELWIN

What am I thinking?

(King Elwin reaches for the axe, peering up at Pride.)

Maybe I should chop down this tree.

PRIDE

(laughs)

Think again, my old elf friend. I knew you way back when. You and I are kith and kin!

(Pride grabs King Elwin in a bear hug, squeezing. King Elwin yowls with pain.)

ELDER GLORIMER

(waving his staff through the air)

Hasten back to the darkness, Pride, and take your pomposity with you.

(Darla picks up a stick threateningly.)

DARLA

Let him go!

*(Pride chuckles devilishly. King Elwin grimaces in pain
from Pride's grasp. Darla sneaks up behind Pride and
whacks him with the stick. He releases King Elwin, who
falls to the ground, and turns toward Darla. Darla backs
away in fright as Pride paces toward her. Meanwhile, Elder
Glorimer attends to the dazed king.)*

KING ELWIN

(to Elder Glorimer)

I'll be fine. See to Darla.

*(Elder Glorimer springs into action and hits Pride on the
back with his staff, igniting sparks. Pride caterwauls in
pain from the magical blow.)*

ELDER GLORIMER

Depart, Pride, and take your shadow friends with you!

DARLA

Get lost!

KING ELWIN

Go!

*(All three elves attack Pride and, after a struggle, toss him
back into the copse.)*

KING ELWIN

(weak and winded)

Thank you!

ACT V: SCENE 1

ELDER GLORIMER
The Tree! The Tree!

> (King Elwin picks up the axe and chops down the tree in three cuts. Hopping on her feet, Darla claps and cheers as the tree falls.)

ELDER GLORIMER
> (beholding the fallen tree)

God be praised; the Poison Tree is down!

KING ELWIN
I couldn't have done it without you both.

DARLA
Now we can truly rejoice.

ELDER GLORIMER
Now we only need to heal the breach.

DARLA/KING ELWIN/ELDER GLORIMER
> (feeling daunted)

The breach!

(BLACKOUT)

Act V: Scene 2

(Pastor Braun, Hans, and Fritz stand beside the tree with the carven heart that reads "Lise plus Christof," but the branches are bare.)

PASTOR BRAUN

(pointing)

See that country chapel through the trees? That's where I shepherd my sheep, or try to. Sheep can be incredibly obstinate creatures.

HANS

Then Fritz would fit right in.

FRITZ

Me?

(Pastor Braun laughs. Fritz looks up at the sky and holds out his hands.)

FRITZ

I can't believe it! Just yesterday was summer, and now it's snowing!

Act V: Scene 2

PASTOR BRAUN

This eventful year has passed swiftly.

(blowing into his palms as if it's cold)

You did say you'd attend the morning service. I could use more voices in the choir.

HANS

Well, we can't just stand outside while everybody else sings and prays. That would be totally idiotic.

PASTOR BRAUN

Wonderful!

FRITZ

(reading the tree carving)

"Lise plus Christof." This tree looks familiar. I know where we are! My cousin, Otto, lives just down the road from that chapel.

PASTOR BRAUN

Perhaps you'll see him at the morning service.

(A church bell chimes.)

PASTOR BRAUN

There's the bell! Why don't you run ahead, sign the guest book, check out the Christmas tree, warm up by the wood stove, and let the greeters show you around? I'll stay here and say hello to whoever is approaching through the trees.

*(Hans and Fritz exit toward the chapel.
King Elwin [with axe in hand], Elder Glorimer, and Darla
approach from the left as King Twinklebee, Buttercup,
Bluebell, and Fawn approach from the right.)*

KING TWINKLEBEE

King Elwin, it's good to see you, looking well, and with an axe in hand. You've always been a faithful steward of your woods. Were you able to chop down the Poison Tree?

(King Twinklebee and King Elwin shake hands.)

KING ELWIN

Greetings, fairy liege. Thankfully, yes, after struggling with some shadows, and with a little help from family and friends, I felled the tree, though we've yet to heal the breach.

KING TWINKLEBEE

That's why we're here, except for she who is lost to me.

(Trixie and the Moth Queen emerge from the trees.)

TRIXIE

Here I am!

THE MOTH QUEEN

I hope we're not too late.

PASTOR BRAUN

You're right on time. Welcome, all.

THE MOTH QUEEN

After crossing a few mountains and braving a few storms, Trixie found shelter with me. We had much catching up to do.

KING TWINKLEBEE

(to Trixie)

I'm glad you're safe, Trixie, but I'm still angry. You ran away with that bear!

TRIXIE

(to Twinklebee)

To every story, there are two sides.

BUTTERCUP

Or three.

BLUEBELL

Or four.

FAWN

Or five.

(Babik emerges through the trees.)

BABIK

(sheepishly)

Or more.

(Elder Glorimer sighs and shakes his head with amused dismay.)

TRIXIE

(to King Twinklebee)

I couldn't forsake Babik to the cruelty of his captors. But I knew you wouldn't let me keep him. I knew you'd just say, "No, he'll track mud in the castle."

KING TWINKLEBEE

That's no excuse.

ELDER GLORIMER

Now hold on. Maybe this controversy is all for naught. Maybe it's alright to fall in love with an animal. Pastor Braun?

PASTOR BRAUN

(reflecting)

I did once have a pet cat I loved dearly, and my girlfriend at the time tolerated her quite well.

ELDER GLORIMER

Then it's settled. It's alright to fall in love with an animal.

TRIXIE

Yet you abandoned me in the woods, Babik. I searched everywhere but found only shadows. Why did you leave me?

BABIK

(sheepishly peering at his hands)

When I saw my sin . . . I just couldn't face you.

TRIXIE

How do you think I felt? My wimple was none too white.

(Diogenes emerges through the trees and joins the throng.)

KING ELWIN

Diogenes, what a pleasant surprise. It's been eons.

(King Elwin and Diogenes shake hands.)

DIOGENES

Hello, King Elwin, everybody.

(scanning the assembly)

I seek the Righteous One, the one who cannot be found.

PASTOR BRAUN

But he can be found by those who seek him. I know a place where we can meet him, Jesus Christ, the Lord.

DIOGENES

(to Pastor Braun)

Then what are we waiting for? Lead on!

DARLA

To the chapel!

ELDER GLORIMER

(nodding at King Elwin)

Let's heal the breach!

(All head toward the chapel through the trees.)

(Blackout)

Act V: Scene 3 (Optional)

(All characters, with or without choir boys/girls, sing the contemporary version of "I Heard the Bells on Christmas Day," affirming the timeless message of peace.)